Published by Ice House Books

Copyright © 2019 Ice House Books
Illustrations by Jocelyn Kao
Original text by Lewis Carroll

Ice House Books is an imprint of Half Moon Bay Limited
The Ice House, 124 Walcot Street, Bath, BA1 5BG
www.icehousebooks.co.uk

This is a celebration of the novel and not intended as a direct
replica of the original text. Excerpts have been selected and some
text has been omitted to create a collection of well-loved scenes.

ISBN 978-1-912867-33-2

Printed in China

CLASSIC MOMEN

Alice

Wonder

LEWIS CARR

CLASSIC MOMENTS FROM

Alice In Wonderland

LEWIS CARROLL

ICE HOUSE BOOKS

From Chapter I

Alice was considering in her own mind, (as well as she could, for the hot day made her feel very sleepy and stupid), whether the pleasure of making a daisy-chain would be worth the trouble of getting up and picking the daisies, when suddenly a white rabbit with pink eyes ran close by her.

There was nothing so very remarkable in that; nor did Alice think it so very much out of the way to hear the Rabbit say to itself ...

"Oh dear! Oh dear! I shall be too late!"

(when she thought it over afterwards, it occurred to her that she ought to have wondered at this, but at the time it all seemed quite natural); but when the Rabbit actually took a watch out of its waistcoat-pocket, and looked at it, and then hurried on, Alice started to her feet, for it flashed across her mind that she had never before seen a rabbit with either a waistcoat-pocket or a watch to take out of it, and, burning with curiosity, she ran across the field after it, and was just in time to see it pop down a large rabbit-hole under the hedge.

In another moment down went Alice after it, never once considering how in the world she was to get out again.

[...]

"Oh, how I wish I could shut up like a telescope! I think I could, if I only knew how to begin." For, you see, so many out-of-the-way things had happened lately that Alice had begun to think that ...

... very few things indeed were really impossible.

There seemed to be no use in waiting by the little door, so she went back to the table, half hoping she might find another key on it, or at any rate a book of rules for shutting people up like telescopes: this time she found a little bottle on it, ("which certainly was not here before," said Alice), and tied round the neck of the bottle was a paper label with the words "DRINK ME" beautifully printed on it in large letters.

[...]

"What a curious feeling!" said Alice, "I must be shutting up like a telescope."

And so it was indeed: she was now only ten inches high, and her face brightened up at the thought that she was now the right size for going through the little door into that lovely garden.

But, alas for poor Alice! When she got to the door, she found she had forgotten the little golden key, and when she went back to the table for it, she found she could not possibly reach it.

Soon her eye fell on a little glass box that was lying under the table: she opened it, and found in it a very small cake, on which the words ...

"EAT ME"

... were beautifully marked in currants. "Well, I'll eat it," said Alice, "and if it makes me grow smaller, I can creep under the door; so either way I'll get into the garden, and I don't care which happens!"

She ate a little bit, and said anxiously to herself "Which way? Which way?" holding her hand on top of her head to feel which way it was growing, and she was quite surprised to find that she remained the same size: to be sure, this is what generally happens when one eats cake, but Alice had got so much into the way of expecting nothing but out-of-the-way things to happen, that it seemed quite dull and stupid for life to go on in the common way.

So she set to work, and very soon finished off the cake.

"Curiouser and curiouser!"

From Chapter II

After a time she heard a little pattering of feet in the distance, and she hastily dried her eyes to see what was coming. It was the White Rabbit returning, splendidly dressed, with a pair of white kid gloves in one hand and a large fan in the other: he came trotting along in a great hurry, muttering to himself as he came, "Oh, the Duchess, the Duchess! Oh! won't she be savage if I've kept her waiting!" Alice felt so desperate that she was ready to ask help of anyone; so, when the Rabbit came near her, she began, in a low, timid voice, "If you please, sir—" The Rabbit started violently, dropped the white kid gloves and the fan, and skurried away into the darkness as hard as he could go.

Alice took up the fan and gloves, and, as the hall was very hot, she kept fanning herself all the time she went on talking: "Dear, dear! How queer everything is to-day! And yesterday things went on just as usual. I wonder if I've been changed in the night? Let me think: was I the same when I got up this morning? I almost think I can remember feeling a little different. But if I'm not the same, the next question is ...

"Who in the world am I? Ah, that's the great puzzle!"

[...]

"I never was so small as this before, never! And I declare it's too bad, that it is!"

As she said these words her foot slipped, and in another moment, splash! she was up to her chin in salt water. Her first idea was that she had somehow fallen into the sea, "and in that case I can go back by railway," she said to herself. However she soon made out that she was in the pool of tears ...

... which she had cried when she was nine feet high.

"It was much pleasanter at home," thought poor Alice, "when one wasn't always growing larger and smaller, and being ordered about by mice and rabbits. I almost wish I hadn't gone down that rabbit-hole–and yet–and yet–it's rather curious, you know, this sort of life! I do wonder what can have happened to me! When I used to read fairy tales, I fancied that kind of thing never happened, and now here I am in the middle of one!"

From Chapter V

The Caterpillar and Alice looked at each other for some time in silence: at last the Caterpillar took the hookah out of its mouth, and addressed her in a languid, sleepy voice.

"Who are you?" said the Caterpillar.

This was not an encouraging opening for a conversation. Alice replied, rather shyly, "I—I hardly know, sir, just at present—at least I know who I was when I got up this morning, but I think …

I must have been changed several times since then."

"What do you mean by that? Said the Caterpillar sternly. "Explain yourself!"

"I can't explain myself, I'm afraid, sir," said Alice, "because I'm not myself, you see."

From Chapter VI

"Please, would you tell me," said Alice, a little timidly, for she was not quite sure whether it was good manners for her to speak first, "why your cat grins like that?"

"It's a Cheshire Cat," said the Duchess, "and that's why. Pig!"

She said the last word with such sudden violence that Alice quite jumped; but she saw in another moment that it was addressed to the baby, and not to her, so she took courage, and went on again: —

"I didn't know that Cheshire cats always grinned; in fact ...

I didn't know that cats could grin."

"They all can," said the Duchess; "and most of 'em do."

"I don't know of any that do," Alice said very politely, feeling quite pleased to have got into a conversation.

"You don't know much," said the Duchess; "and that's a fact."

[...]

"If everybody minded their own business," said the Duchess in a hoarse growl, "the world would go round a deal faster than it does."

"Which would not be an advantage," said Alice, who felt very glad to get an opportunity of showing off a little of her knowledge. "Just think what work it would make with the day and night! You see the earth takes twenty-four hours to turn round on its axis—"

"Talking of axes," said the Duchess, "chop off her head!"

[...]

"Cheshire Puss," she began, rather timidly, as she did not at all know whether it would like the name: however, it only grinned a little wider. "Come, it's pleased so far," thought Alice, and she went on, "Would you tell me, please, which way I ought to walk from here?"

"That depends a good deal on where you want to get to," said the Cat.

"I don't much care where—" said Alice.

"Then it doesn't matter which way you walk,"

said the Cat.

"—so long as I get somewhere," Alice added as an explanation.

"Oh, you're sure to do that," said the Cat, "if you only walk long enough."

[...]

"What sort of people live about here?"

"In that direction," the Cat said, waving its right paw around, "lives a Hatter: and in that direction," waving the other paw, "lives a March Hare. Visit either you like: they're both mad."

"But I don't want to go among mad people," Alice remarked.

"Oh, you can't help that," said the Cat:

"We're all mad here. I'm mad. You're mad."

"How do you know I'm mad?" said Alice.

"You must be," said the Cat, "or you wouldn't have come here."

"I wish you wouldn't keep appearing and vanishing so suddenly: you make one quite giddy."

"All right," said the Cat; and this time it vanished quite slowly, beginning with the end of the tail, and ending with the grin, which remained some time after the rest of it had gone.

"Well! I've often seen a cat without a grin," thought Alice; "but a grin without a cat! It's the most curious thing I ever saw in all my life!"

From Chapter VII

"Why is a raven like a writing-desk?"

"Come, we shall have some fun now!" thought Alice. "I'm glad they've begun asking riddles—I believe I can guess that," she added aloud.

"Do you mean that you think you can find out the answer to it?" said the March Hare.

"Exactly so," said Alice.

"Then you should say what you mean," the March Hare went on.

"I do," Alice hastily replied ...

"at least ~ at least I mean what I say ~ that's the same thing, you know."

"Not the same thing a bit!" said the Hatter.

[…]

"Have you guessed the riddle yet? the Hatter said, turning to Alice again.

"No, I give it up," Alice replied: "what's the answer?"

"I haven't the slightest idea," said the Hatter.

"Nor I," said the March Hare.

Alice sighed wearily. "I think you might do something better with the time," she said, "then wasting it in asking riddles that have no answers."

"If you knew Time as well as I do," said the Hatter …

"you wouldn't talk about wasting it. It's him."

"I don't know what you mean," said Alice.

"Of course you don't!" the Hatter said, tossing his head contemptuously. "I dare say you never even spoke to Time!"

"Perhaps not," Alice cautiously replied: "but I know I have to beat time when I learn music."

"Ah! that accounts for it," said the Hatter. "He won't stand beating. Now, if you only kept on good terms with him, he'd do almost anything you liked with the clock. For instance, suppose it were nine o'clock in the morning, just time to begin lessons: you'd only have to whisper a hint to Time, and round goes the clock in a twinkling! Half-past one, time for dinner!"

From Chapter VIII

A large rose-tree stood near the entrance of the garden: the roses growing on it were white, but there were three gardeners at it, busily painting them red. Alice thought this a very curious thing, and she went nearer to watch them, and just as she came up to them she heard one of them say, "Look out now, Five! Don't go splashing paint over me like that!"

"I couldn't help it," said Five in a sulky tone; "Seven jogged my elbow."

On which Seven looked up and said, "That's right, Five! Always lay the blame on others!"

[...]

"Would you tell me, please," said Alice, a little timidly, "why you are painting those roses?"

Five and Seven said nothing, but looked at Two. Two began, in a low voice, "Why, the fact is, you see, Miss, this here ought to have been a red rose-tree, and we put a white one in by mistake, if the Queen was to find out ...

... we should all have our heads cut off, you know.

So you see, Miss, we're doing our best, afore she comes, to—" At this moment Five, who had been anxiously looking across the garden, called out "The Queen! The Queen!" and the three gardeners instantly threw themselves flat upon their faces.

[...]

"And who are these?" said the Queen, pointing to the three gardeners who were lying round the rose-tree; for you see, as they were lying on their faces, and the pattern on their backs was the same as the rest of the pack, she could not tell whether they were gardeners, or soldiers, or courtiers, or three of her own children.

"How should I know?" said Alice, surprised at her own courage. "It's no business of mine."

The Queen turned crimson with fury, and, after glaring at her for a moment like a wild beast, began screaming ...

"Off with her head! Off—"

"Nonsense!" said Alice, very loudly and decidedly, and the Queen was silent.

[...]

Alice thought she had never seen such a curious croquet-ground in her life: it was all ridges and furrows; the croquet-balls were live hedgehogs ...

... *and the mallets live flamingoes* ...

... and the soldiers had to double themselves up and stand on their hands and feet, to make the arches.

The chief difficulty Alice found at first was in managing her flamingo: she succeeded in getting its body tucked away, comfortably enough, under her arm, with its legs hanging down, but generally, just as she had got its neck nicely straightened out, and was going to give the hedgehog a blow with its head, it would twist itself round and look up into her face, with such a puzzled expression that she could not help bursting out laughing.

From Chapter IX

"Everything's got a moral, if only you can find it." And the Duchess squeezed herself up closer to Alice's side as she spoke.

Alice did not much like her keeping so close to her: first, because the Duchess was very ugly, and secondly, because she was exactly the right height to rest her chin on Alice's shoulder, and it was an uncomfortably sharp chin. However, she did not like to be rude, so she bore it as well as she could. "The game's going on rather better now," she said by way of keeping up the conversation a little.

"'Tis so," said the Duchess: "and the moral of that is—

Oh, 'tis love, that makes the world go round!'"

"Somebody said," Alice whispered, "that it's done by everybody minding their own business!"

"Ah, well! It means much the same thing," said the Duchess, digging her sharp little chin into Alice's shoulder as she added, "and the moral of *that* is—'Take care of sense, and the sounds will take care of themselves.'"

From Chapter X

"Come, let's hear some of your adventures."

"I could tell you my adventures—beginning from this morning," said Alice a little timidly:

"But it's no use going back to yesterday ...

because I was a different person then."

"Explain all that," said the Mock Turtle.

"No, no! the adventures first," said the Gryphon in an impatient tone: "explanations take such a dreadful time."

So Alice began telling them her adventures from the time when she first saw the White Rabbit.

"It's all about as curious as it can be," said the Gryphon.

"It all came different!" the Mock Turtle repeated thoughtfully. "I should like to hear her try and repeat something now. Tell her to begin." He looked at the Gryphon as if he thought it had some kind of authority over Alice.

"Stand up and repeat ''Tis the voice of the sluggard,'" said the Gryphon.

"How the creatures order one about, and make one repeat lessons!" thought Alice. "I might just as well be at school at once."

Alice had never been in a court of justice before, but she had read about them in books, and she was quite pleased to find that she knew the name of nearly everything there. "That's the judge," she said to herself, "because of his great wig."

The judge, by the way, was the King, and as he wore his crown over the wig, (look at the frontispiece if you want to see how he did it), he did not look at all comfortable, and it was certainly not becoming.

"Sentence first—verdict afterwards."

"Stuff and nonsense!"

said Alice loudly. "The idea of having the sentence first!"

"Hold your tongue!" said the Queen, turning purple.

"I won't!" said Alice.

"Off with her head!" the Queen shouted at the top of her voice. Nobody moved.

"Who cares for you?" said Alice, (she had grown to her full size by this time.) "You're nothing but a pack of cards!"

At this the whole pack rose up into the air, and came flying down upon her; she gave a little scream, half of fright and half of anger, and tried to beat them off, and found herself lying on the bank, with her head in the lap of her sister, who was gently brushing away some dead leaves that had fluttered down from the trees onto her face.

From Chapter XII

"Wake up, Alice dear!" said her sister; "why, what a long sleep you've had!"

"Oh, I've had such a curious dream!" said Alice, and she told her sister, as well as she could remember them, all these strange Adventures of hers that you have just been reading about; and when she had finished, her sister kissed her, and said ...

"It was a curious dream, dear, certainly...

but now run in to your tea; it's getting late."

So Alice got up and ran off, thinking while she ran, as well she might, what a wonderful dream it had been.

But her sister sat still just as she left her, leaning her head on her hand, watching the setting sun, and thinking of little Alice and all her wonderful Adventures.

So she sat on, with closed eyes, and half believed herself in Wonderland, though she knew she had but to open them again and all would change to dull reality — the grass would be only rustling in the wind, and the pool rippling to the waving of the reeds — the rattling teacups would change to tinkling sheep-bells, and the Queen's shrill cries to the voice of the shepherd boy — and the sneeze of the baby, the shriek of the Gryphon, and all the other queer noises, would change (she knew) to the confused clamor of the barn farm-yard — while the lowing of the cattle in the distance would take place of the Mock Turtle's heavy sobs.

Lastly, she pictured to herself how this same little sister of hers would, in the after-time, be herself a grown woman; and how she would keep, through all her riper years, the simple and loving heart of her childhood: and how she would gather about her other little children, and make their eyes bright and eager with many a strange tale, perhaps even ...

... with the dream of Wonderland of long-ago...

... and how she would feel with all their simple sorrows, and find a pleasure in all their simple joys, remembering her own child-life, and the happy summer days.